The Petal Fairies

For the sparkling Carrie Morling,
with love

Special thanks to
Sue Mongredien

ORCHARD BOOKS
338 Euston Road, London NW1 3BH
Orchard Books Australia
Level 17/207 Kent Street, Sydney, NSW 2000
A Paperback Original

First published in 2007 by Orchard Books
Rainbow Magic is a registered trademark of Working Partners Limited.
Series created by Working Partners Limited, London W6 OQT

Text © Working Partners Limited 2007
Cover illustrations © Georgie Ripper 2007
Inside illustrations © Orchard Books 2007

A CIP catalogue record for this book is available
from the British Library.

ISBN 978 1 84616 458 3
1 3 5 7 9 10 8 6 4 2

Printed in Great Britain

Orchard Books is a division of Hachette Children's Books

www.orchardbooks.co.uk

Pippa the Poppy Fairy

by Daisy Meadows

ORCHARD BOOKS

www.rainbowmagic.co.uk

I need the magic petals' powers,
To give my castle garden flowers.
And so I use my magic well
To work against the fairies' spell.

From my wand ice magic flies,
Frosty bolt through fairy skies.
And this crafty spell I weave
To bring the petals back to me.

Contents

Special Delivery

"I love Blossom Hall!" Kirsty Tate
sighed happily, as she finished off
a delicious bowl of fruit and cereal.

She was sitting on the sunny terrace
of the hotel restaurant with her best
friend Rachel Walker and their parents.
The two families were spending a week
at the old Tudor house which was now

a hotel, over the Easter holidays.
The sky was blue, and the pink
and white cherry trees in the gardens
were in full bloom.

"It's lovely," Rachel agreed.

"Did you find the Fairy Garden
yesterday?" Mrs Tate asked.

Rachel and Kirsty nodded.

"It was magic!" Rachel said, and
she and Kirsty grinned at each other.

The two girls shared a very special secret. On a previous holiday they had become friends with the fairies. Yesterday, in the hotel garden, they had met Tia the Tulip Fairy, and begun a whole new fairy adventure.

"What do you two want to do today?" asked Mr Walker.

"We'd like to explore inside Blossom Hall this morning," Rachel said eagerly.

"I can't wait to look around," Kirsty added. "Mum, please can we—"

"Yes, you can leave the table if you've finished," Mrs Tate laughed.

"All the more bacon and eggs for me!" Mr Walker said teasingly as the girls got up.

Laughing, Rachel and Kirsty left the restaurant and set off down one of the winding corridors, looking at the pictures on the walls.

One of them showed a pretty village green. "That's Blossom Village, isn't it?" Kirsty said.

Rachel nodded. They had driven through the village to reach Blossom Hall.

"This is Blossom Hall," Rachel remarked, pausing in front of another print. "It says it was built in 1550!"

Next to the picture of Blossom Hall hung an oil painting of a field scattered with wildflowers: scarlet poppies, golden buttercups and blue cornflowers.

"It's lucky they're only painted flowers," Rachel sighed, "or they'd all be dying now that the Petal Fairies' magic petals have been stolen!"

The girls had learned that Jack Frost
was causing trouble for the fairies. He
had sent his goblin servants to steal the
seven magic petals and, without them,
flowers in Fairyland and in the human
world couldn't bloom properly. The
Petal Fairies had tried to get their
petals back, but in the struggle between
their magic and Jack Frost's icy spell,
the petals had spun out of sight into the
human world. Jack Frost had sent his
goblins to bring them back, but Rachel
and Kirsty were determined to find
them first and return them to Fairyland.

"At least we managed to find Tia's
Tulip Petal yesterday," Kirsty said.
"I wonder if we'll find another magic
petal today."

"I hope so," Rachel replied.

The girls arrived at the hotel reception, a spacious hallway with stained glass windows and a large mahogany table with a display of flowers. At that moment the main doors opened and a man in blue overalls came in, carrying an enormous basket of flowers.

"Hello, Bill," said Jenny, the receptionist. "Can you put the flowers in their usual place, please?"

Bill went over to the table, removed the old basket of dying flowers and put the new one in its place. Rachel thought the flowers were beautiful, especially the huge poppies. Their silky petals were gorgeous rich shades of red and orange, which contrasted with their jet-black centres.

Bill went over to the reception desk, and began to discuss next week's order with Jenny. Rachel and Kirsty could see that he had Petal Perfection Flower Shop printed on the back of his overalls.

"That's the flower shop in Blossom Village," Kirsty said to Rachel. "We drove past it on our way here."

"We'll do our best, Jenny," Bill was saying, "but we're having a lot of problems at the moment. Our flowers are dying very quickly and we don't know why!"

Kirsty sighed. "It's because six of the seven magic petals are still missing," she whispered to Rachel. "New flowers won't grow, and the ones which have already bloomed don't last very long at all."

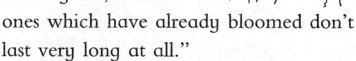

Rachel nodded sadly in agreement.

Bill took out his notebook. "I'll go and get the rest of the order from the hotel manager," he said, and hurried off.

Rachel stared at the flowers Bill had just brought in. She could see that some of them were already wilting even though they were fresh from the flower shop. Suddenly her heart skipped a beat. "Kirsty," she whispered, clutching her friend's arm, "I just saw some red fairy sparkles shoot out of the basket!"

"Oh!" Kirsty looked thrilled.

The two girls hurried over to the flowers. As they reached them, there was another shower of crimson sparkles, and a tiny fairy zoomed out from the middle of a scarlet poppy.

A Window Seat

"Oh, girls, I am glad to see you!"
Pippa the Poppy Fairy exclaimed,
dancing through the air towards Kirsty
and Rachel. She wore a floaty scarlet
dress, a matching hairband and tiny
ballet shoes decorated with poppies.

"Hello, Pippa," Kirsty said excitedly.
"Do you think your magic petal's here?"

Pippa's glittering wings drooped a little. "No, it's not here," she said sadly. "But I know where it is!" "Tell us, Pippa," Rachel urged. "Well, I was in the flower shop in Blossom Village, looking for my petal," Pippa explained. "But I was so busy looking that I got swept up in this basket of flowers and carried out of the shop!"

"So that's how you arrived here," said Kirsty.

Pippa nodded. "And I'm glad you and Rachel found me," she added, "because I didn't know where I was going to end up. But I'm sure I saw my magic petal just as I got carried out of the shop, so I must get back there as quickly as possible!"

Kirsty and Rachel glanced round cautiously. The reception area was getting very busy as people passed through on their way to and from breakfast.

"Let's go over to the window seat and think of a plan," Rachel suggested.

Pippa nodded and dived into Rachel's pocket as the girls hurried over to the large bay window and sat

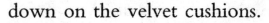

down on the velvet cushions.

"Look at my poor poppies," Pippa said, peeping out and pointing at the

basket of flowers. Rachel and Kirsty could see that the delicate flowerheads were already starting to droop.

"I must get my magic petal back so that the poppies, and the other red flowers – which are all controlled by the Poppy Petal – can grow beautifully again!"

"The tulips are lovely," Kirsty remarked, gazing at the orange flowers which were blooming brightly. "That's because we found Tia the Tulip Fairy's petal yesterday."

Pippa nodded. "But only when we have all the magic petals safely back in Fairyland, will all the flowers in the human world be able to grow properly again," she pointed out.

"We'll find them," Rachel said in
a determined voice.

"Don't forget that the
goblins have a wand full
of Jack Frost's icy magic
to help them," Pippa
said with a shiver.
"We must be
careful, girls."

Kirsty nodded,
but just then
a movement
outside the window
caught her eye. She
turned to look. There,
to her dismay, was a big,
green goblin running at full
speed across the hotel courtyard.

"Look, it's a goblin!" Kirsty gasped.

The goblin was running towards
a white van parked outside the
hotel. Petal Perfection
Flower Shop was painted
on the side of the van
in curly green letters,
and its back doors
were wide open.
As the girls and
Pippa watched,
the goblin skidded
to a halt and
waved his arms.
Immediately
a whole band of
goblins raced out of the
shrubbery. One of them
was carrying the glittering icy
wand which Jack Frost had given them.

"There are lots of them!" Pippa whispered anxiously as the goblins began climbing onto each other's shoulders to get inside the van.

"They're looking for the magic petal," Rachel replied.

Pippa shook her head. "It was left behind in the shop; I'm sure of it," she said.

"Look at what the goblins are doing now!" Kirsty remarked, frowning.

All the goblins had climbed inside the delivery van. The girls and Pippa couldn't see them, but what they could see were flowers flying out of the open doors of the van. Daffodils, tulips and other flowers came hurtling out, landing in a heap in the courtyard.

"Oh!" Pippa cried, clasping her hands together in horror. "How can they treat those beautiful flowers like that? We must stop them!"

"Yes, and quickly, too," Rachel added anxiously. "Before the delivery man sees them!"

Goblins Get a Ride

Quickly Pippa nestled down inside Rachel's pocket again, and the two girls jumped up. But they were too late! Bill was already at the hotel door, waving goodbye to Jenny.

"I'll take your order straight back to the shop," he was saying. "Goodbye."

Kirsty and Rachel glanced at each

other in dismay as Bill went out. They
rushed after him into the courtyard and
were just in time to see him picking up
the flowers which were scattered
on the ground.

"What's happened here?" Bill was
muttering. "Surely the wind couldn't
have blown the flowers out of my van.
I must have knocked some flowers over
when I got the hotel's order out."

The girls watched as Bill carefully loaded the flowers back into the van and then closed the doors. They couldn't see a single goblin though.

"Do you think the goblins jumped out before Bill got there?" whispered Rachel.

"I don't know," Kirsty said, frowning.

Bill jumped into the van and, with a cheery wave at the girls, he drove off.

Petal
Perfection
Flower Shop

"Kirsty!" Rachel cried suddenly.
"Look at the back of the van!"

Kirsty's heart sank. There, grinning
at them from the back
windows of the van,
were the goblins!
They were
pulling faces at
Pippa and the
girls, sticking
their tongues
out and
waggling their
fingers behind their
ears. As the van pulled
away, they waved a cheeky goodbye,
looking very pleased with themselves.

"The goblins are on their way to the
flower shop," Rachel groaned.

"They might even find Pippa's magic petal!" added Kirsty.

"And I don't even want to think about all the damage those naughty goblins could do in the flower shop," Pippa said. "Girls, we must go after them!"

"I'm sure our parents will let us go to the village," said Kirsty. "It's only at the end of the hotel drive."

"But we'll need a reason to go to the flower shop," Rachel pointed out.

Kirsty nodded thoughtfully, but at that moment she noticed a crumpled piece of paper lying on the gravel driveway. She picked it up.

35

"What's that?" asked Rachel curiously.

Kirsty smoothed the paper flat. Across the top, the words "Petal Perfection Flower Shop, High Street, Blossom Village" were printed. There was some writing underneath.

"One basket of pink roses, one bouquet of pink and white tulips,"

Kirsty read out. "This is the hotel's order for next week. Bill must have dropped it." "Perfect!" Rachel beamed happily. "We can go into the flower shop to return it."

Pippa was so excited, she twirled herself out of Rachel's pocket in a shower of red sparkles. "Hurry, girls!" she said eagerly. "You'd better go and ask your parents' permission."

"I'll do that," Rachel replied. "Maybe we could borrow some of the hotel bikes, Kirsty. The driveway's really long, and it would be much quicker than walking."

"Good idea," Kirsty agreed. The girls knew that Blossom Hall kept bicycles for guests to use to explore the countryside. "I'll ask Jenny."

"I'll wait here," Pippa said, zooming out of sight behind a nearby shrub.

Rachel hurried off to find their parents while Kirsty went back into reception.

"Of course you can borrow some bikes, Kirsty," Jenny said kindly. "Come with me."

The receptionist took Kirsty to
a large garage behind the hotel where
the bikes were stored. She gave Kirsty
padlocks and chains for the bikes, and
two safety helmets. Then she helped
Kirsty wheel the bikes round to the
hotel driveway, before returning to
the reception desk.

"That was quick!" Pippa whispered, popping out of the shrubbery as soon as Jenny had disappeared.

"And here comes Rachel," said Kirsty.

"We can go," Rachel announced, "but we can't leave the village and we must be back in an hour."

Pippa immediately flew into the basket on the front of Rachel's bike and settled herself comfortably inside. "Let's go," she cried. "We haven't a moment to lose!"

Petal Pandemonium

The girls put on their helmets, climbed onto the bikes and pedalled off as fast as they could go. It was a very long and winding driveway, and soon they were panting hard.

"Look at the hedgerows," Pippa pointed out, as the gates at the end of the drive finally came into sight. "Even my beautiful wild poppies are dying!"

Rachel and Kirsty could see that the scarlet poppies were indeed wilting. Not only that, but many of the primroses and cowslips in the hedgerows were dying too, even though they were supposed to be in full bloom.

"We must get all the magic petals back," said Rachel in a determined voice, forcing herself to pedal faster.

Petal Perfection Flower Shop was in the high street near the village green.

"Let's hope the goblins haven't found my magic petal yet," Pippa whispered, as she slipped into Rachel's pocket.

Kirsty and Rachel locked up their bikes, took off their helmets and hurried into the shop. There was nobody inside except a woman with long dark hair tied up in a ponytail. She was standing behind the counter, frowning, as she put blue irises and yellow roses together in a beautiful arrangement.

"Oh, dear!" the woman sighed as she laid aside a drooping rose. Then she spotted Rachel and Kirsty. "Hello," she said, looking flustered. "Sorry, I didn't see you there. I'm having such problems with my flowers."

Rachel and Kirsty glanced around the shop. They could see that many of the flowers on display in tall silver vases were looking sad and bedraggled. The poppies were especially bad, their large heads drooping and their fragile petals brown at the edges.

"We've got lots of orders to fill.
I don't know how I'm going to
manage," the woman went
on. "Anyway, I'm Kate.
My husband, Bill,
and I own the
shop. What can
I do for you?"

"We're staying at
Blossom Hall," Kirsty
explained, holding out the piece of
paper. "Bill came this morning with
the flowers, but he accidentally dropped
next week's order when he left."

Kate beamed at them. "Oh, thank
you, girls," she said gratefully. "Bill
got back a little while ago, but he's
just popped out in the van to deliver
another order."

Rachel and Kirsty
glanced at each
other, wondering
if the goblins had
managed to
escape from the
van and get into
the shop.

"I must finish this
bouquet for a new mum," Kate
explained. "But why don't you pop
through to the back room and choose
some flowers to take home with you
as a thank you?"

"Yes, please," Rachel and Kirsty
chorused.

Kate pointed at a door behind the
counter. "It's through there," she said.
"Just help yourselves."

"Perfect!" Pippa whispered, popping her head out of Rachel's pocket as soon as they had closed the door behind them. "Now we'll have a chance to look for my magic petal!"

"And maybe the goblins, too," added Kirsty.

Quickly the girls and Pippa hurried into the back room.

"Oh, no," Rachel groaned, coming to a halt in the doorway. "The goblins are here!"

The goblins were running around,
frantically looking for the magic
petal, and the room was
a complete mess.
Pippa and the girls
stared in dismay at
the buckets of
flowers that had
been kicked over,
and at the floor
awash with water.
There were stray
petals and leaves
everywhere.

But the goblins were
having great fun! One had
got himself wrapped in a roll
of pink, flowery wrapping paper. He
looked like an Egyptian mummy, with

just his big green ears, nose and feet sticking out. Another had draped himself in multi-coloured ribbons and was swinging another long ribbon over his head like a lasso. The goblin with the wand had a large daffodil stuck behind each ear and a garland of daisies round his neck.

"I don't think they've found the petal yet," Kirsty whispered. She, Rachel and Pippa couldn't help laughing at the goblins' antics, even though they were horrified by the mess.

"No, they're having too much fun!" Rachel replied. "Look, one's got stuck!"

The biggest goblin was upside-down in an empty flower bucket, his legs waving in the air. He was yelling loudly, but his voice was 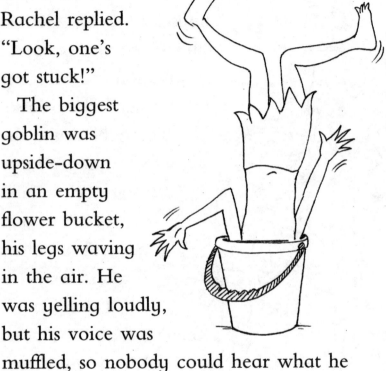 muffled, so nobody could hear what he was saying.

Pippa and the girls watched as two other goblins grabbed his legs and yanked him out.

As his head came out of the bucket, the girls could see that he was grinning. "I've found the magic petal!" he shouted triumphantly.

Ice Magic

Rachel, Kirsty and Pippa stared in horror as the goblin held up a beautiful scarlet poppy petal.

"I'm going to take it straight to Jack Frost!" he boasted.

"No, I want to!" one of the others yelled. All the other goblins immediately joined in, trying to grab the fragile petal.

Rachel couldn't bear to see the petal in danger of being ripped apart. "Give that back!" she demanded bravely. The goblins all turned to glare at her.

"Shan't!" the biggest goblin sneered. He dashed out of the back door of the shop, immediately followed by all the other goblins.

"We can't follow them or Kate will wonder where we've gone," Rachel said. "We'd better go out the front way."

"Can you clean up
this mess, Pippa?"
asked Kirsty.

Quickly Pippa
waved her
wand and
a shower of fairy
sparkles magically
cleared up the whole
room, rolling up the wrapping paper
and ribbons and putting the flowers
back into their buckets.

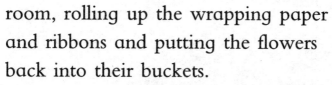

"I can't make the wilting flowers
bloom properly, though, without my
magic petal," Pippa sighed, whizzing
into Rachel's pocket.

The two girls raced back into
the shop.

Kate looked at them in surprise.

"Didn't you find any flowers you liked?" she asked.

"We, er, just remembered something we have to do in the village first," Kirsty stammered.

"We'll come back later to collect some flowers, if that's OK," added Rachel.

"That's fine," Kate replied.

Quickly the girls unlocked their bikes and pedalled round to the back of the store. "There they go!" Rachel shouted, catching a glimpse of the goblins running into the park.

The girls pedalled after them. But by the time they had cycled into the park, the goblins were nowhere to be seen.

"They must be here somewhere," Kirsty said. She gazed around as they came to a halt underneath an oak tree. She could see trees and flowerbeds, and a hill nearby, but no goblins.

Ssshhh!

The sound came from above, startling Kirsty. She glanced up and saw a very odd-looking green branch. Kirsty clapped a hand to her mouth as she realised it was a goblin's leg!

As quietly as she could, she got off her bike, tapped Rachel on the shoulder and pointed upwards. Rachel and Pippa saw the leg and Pippa nodded as Rachel climbed off her bike.

"We'll fly up there and try to grab the petal," Pippa whispered, waving her wand.

Rachel and Kirsty felt a rush of excitement as a cloud of crimson sparkles instantly transformed them into fairies. Silently fluttering their glittering wings, the three friends flew up into the branches of the tree.

"There!" Pippa said softly, pointing with her wand.

The goblins were sitting in a long line on a sturdy branch, their legs dangling. The biggest goblin was at the end, holding the magic petal.

Rachel, who was closest, immediately flew down and made a grab for it. But at the last moment the goblin saw her coming and batted her away.

61

"It's those pesky girls again!" he
called furiously. "Do something!"

"I'll cast a really brilliant spell,"
yelled the goblin with the wand.
"Er, um…"

"Get on with it!" shouted the biggest
goblin as Pippa, Rachel and Kirsty
hovered around him, trying to grab
the petal.

"OK, I've got it," replied the goblin

with the wand. "To escape these girls would be quite nice—" he began, shaking the wand.

"Nice!" shouted the biggest goblin angrily. "It would be brilliant! Not nice!"

"I don't know any words that rhyme with 'brilliant'!" the goblin with the wand said sulkily, and Pippa and the girls laughed.

"To escape these girls would be quite nice," the goblin said again, pointing the wand at the ground. "I demand an icy slide. I mean – a slide of ice!" he finished.

Immediately a huge chute of ice appeared, running from the branches of the tree to the grass below. One by one the goblins leapt on to it with gleeful shrieks and slid to the

ground. The biggest goblin took one last swipe at Pippa and the girls and then followed his friends down the slide.

"They're escaping with the magic petal!" Kirsty cried in dismay as the goblins dashed away.

Petal Perfection

Pippa and the girls flew down from the tree as the goblins fled up the nearby hill. With a deft flick of her wand, Pippa made Rachel and Kirsty human-sized again, and the girls jumped on their bikes.

"After them!" Rachel cried.

The girls zoomed off after the goblins,

Pippa riding in the basket on the front
of Rachel's bike. They reached the foot
of the hill really quickly, but then they
began to struggle.

"It's hard pedalling uphill!" Kirsty
panted, straining to go faster.

Pippa leaned out of the basket
and waved her wand. Dazzling
poppy-red sparkles swirled down
onto both bikes' wheels.

"Oh," Rachel yelled happily, "I'm going much faster now!"

"Me, too," Kirsty agreed. "Thanks, Pippa."

With the help of fairy magic, the girls started gaining on the goblins.

"We're going to overtake the goblins soon," called Rachel.

"Let's try to grab the petal as we pass them," Kirsty suggested.

"Look, the goblin
with the petal is
a little behind
the others,"
Pippa pointed out.

"Kirsty, I'll ride past
on his right-hand side, and you ride
past on his left," Rachel said. "Then
he can't escape."

"Good plan," Kirsty agreed.

As the two girls came up behind the
goblin, Rachel went right and Kirsty

went left. The goblin
was clutching the
petal in his right
hand, and Rachel
reached out for it
as she rode up
behind him.

But at the last moment the goblin spotted her. "Trying to trick me, are you?" he jeered. "You'll have to try harder than that!" And, laughing gleefully, he quickly transferred the petal from his right hand to his left.

But at that very moment, Kirsty sailed past the goblin on his other side, and she reached out and grabbed the petal from his hand while the goblin was still laughing at Rachel.

"Hurrah!" Pippa cried, as they raced
on past the other goblins.

"Hey!" shouted the big goblin
angrily. "Give that magic petal back!"

The other goblins had now realised
what had happened, but they were
too late.

Rachel and Kirsty were speeding
away on their bikes. Behind them, they
could hear the goblins shouting and
arguing with each other because they'd
lost the magic petal.

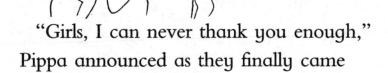

"Girls, I can never thank you enough,"
Pippa announced as they finally came

full circle and arrived back at the park gates. "Now all my poppies and lovely red flowers will bloom beautifully again," she went on. "I must take my precious petal back to Fairyland where it belongs."

She waved her wand over the petal, and it immediately shrank back to its Fairyland size. Pippa took the petal from Kirsty's hand and smiled. "Goodbye, girls," she cried, "and good luck with finding the other petals."

Rachel and Kirsty waved as Pippa disappeared in a burst of poppy-red sparkles.

"Another magic petal found," Kirsty said happily. "Now we'd better get back to Blossom Hall!"

"Ooh, let's collect our flowers from the shop first!" Rachel reminded her.

The girls cycled back to Petal Perfection.

Kate was looking much happier when they walked in. "Hello again, girls," she called cheerfully. "Look at my flowers.

Some of them have perked up no end since you were here before."

Kirsty and Rachel could see that all the poppies and the red flowers were now looking bright and healthy. They grinned at each other.

"Pippa's magic petal is working again already!" Kirsty whispered.

"Tell me which flowers you'd like,"
said Kate. "You've got more to choose
from now."

The girls chose red and orange
poppies, and Kate made them up into
two pretty posies. Then Rachel and
Kirsty said goodbye and cycled back to
Blossom Hall.

"Look, Rachel," said Kirsty, "all
the poppies in the hedgerows are
blooming again!"

"Don't they look beautiful?" Rachel
agreed happily, looking at the silky
crimson heads nodding in the warm
breeze. "I'm so glad we helped another
Petal Fairy today."

The Petal Fairies

Pippa the Poppy Fairy has got
her magic petal back. Now Rachel
and Kirsty must help

Louise the Lily Fairy

Win Rainbow Magic goodies!

In every book in the Rainbow Magic Petal Fairies series
(books 43-49) there is a hidden picture of a petal with a secret letter
in it. Find all seven letters and re-arrange them to make a special
Petal Fairies word, then send it to us. Each month we will put
the entries into a draw and select one winner to receive
a Rainbow Magic Sparkly T-shirt and Goody Bag!

Send your entry on a postcard to Rainbow Magic Fun Day
Competition, Orchard Books, 338 Euston Road, London NW1 3BH.
Australian readers should write to Hachette Children's Books,
Level 17/207 Kent Street, Sydney, NSW 2000.
New Zealand readers should write to Rainbow Magic Competition,
4 Whetu Place, Mairangi Bay, Auckland, NZ. Don't forget to
include your name and address. Only one entry per child.
Final draw: 30th April 2008.

Good luck!

Have you checked out the

website at:
www.rainbowmagic.co.uk

by Daisy Meadows

All priced at £3.99. *Holly the Christmas Fairy, Summer the Holiday Fairy, Stella the Star Fairy, Kylie the Carnival Fairy, Paige the Pantomime Fairy* and *Flora the Fancy Dress Fairy* are priced at £5.99. *The Rainbow Magic Treasury* is priced at £12.99.
Rainbow Magic books are available from all good bookshops, or can be ordered direct from the publisher: Orchard Books, PO BOX 29, Douglas IM99 1BQ
Credit card orders please telephone 01624 836000
or fax 01624 837033 or visit our Internet site: www.wattspub.co.uk
or e-mail: bookshop@enterprise.net for details.

To order please quote title, author and ISBN and your full name and address.
Cheques and postal orders should be made payable to 'Bookpost plc.'
Postage and packing is FREE within the UK
(overseas customers should add £2.00 per book).
Prices and availability are subject to change.

Look out for the Dance Fairies!

BETHANY
THE BALLET FAIRY
978-1-84616-490-3

JADE
THE DISCO FAIRY
978-1-84616-491-0

REBECCA
THE ROCK 'N' ROLL FAIRY
978-1-84616-492-7

TASHA
THE TAP DANCE FAIRY
978-1-84616-493-4

JESSICA
THE JAZZ FAIRY
978-1-84616-495-8

SASKIA
THE SALSA FAIRY
978-1-84616-496-5

IMOGEN
THE ICE DANCE FAIRY
978-1-84616-497-2

Available September 2007